CHARLIE,
A LIFE

Phillip E. Neff

author HOUSE

AuthorHouse™
1663 Liberty Drive
Bloomington, IN 47403
www.authorhouse.com
Phone: 833-262-8899

Published by AuthorHouse 03/13/2023

ISBN: 979-8-8230-0299-8 (sc)
ISBN: 979-8-8230-0298-1 (hc)
ISBN: 979-8-8230-0297-4 (e)

Library of Congress Control Number: 2023904294

Print information available on the last page.

DEDICATION

Charlie is a semi fictitious account of the authors life drawn from facts, dreams and semi-conscious imaginations.

From childhood many of the incidents were taken directly from the antics and machinations of the author with color added to make them more fun.

Many of the incidents were taken directly from life without any deformations or character misalignments.

Many are pure imagination.

Life for all of us has truth and untruths mixed together which enriches our memories as we age. At times we forget which are the truths.

I wrote this tale encompassing both with the rich memories and exaggerations together to bring together what a rich early life I had even through trials and tribulations.

I Dedicate my book to my brother Joseph Lorne whom I never met. (picture of baby) My children Natalie Alexandra Neff, my firstborn and the Apple of my eye. Bravin Garnet Neff, my second born and Andrew Kim Neff our third child who rounded out a wonderful family through the guidance of my wife Yong Cha Neff whom I would be nothing without.

PROLOGUE

Wisps of smoke snaked out of the ground and gathered in a layer about ten feet above the charred remnants of a once proud and lush forest.

Three days had passed since the 40,000 acres had succumbed to Mother Nature's wrath and the army of forest fire fighters assembled to do battle with her.

Fireman Thomas Parks was wending his way up Beaver Snatch Mountain extinguishing hot spots as he went. It was hot dreary and tiresome work mopping up after a big fire. As Thomas crested the ridge line of the modest mountain, he encountered a small stand of young Douglas fir unscathed by the inferno.

The aerial firefighting tankers had saved at least this small part of the once pristine forest.

Breathing a whiff of clean air, the first in over a week, Thomas knew his forest would be reborn.

Thomas was brought fiercely back to reality by a sight that was inexplicable, weird, insane and never encountered by any forest fire fighter at any time in the annals of forest fire fighting. Lifting his radio from his belt he made a call. "Lieutenant Gerard, I think you need to come to the crest of Beaver Snatch, there is something you need to see"

"Can't it wait? I have important business here. Just write up what you find, and we will get to it later."

"No Sir, I really do believe you need to see this and now."

The urgency in the voice of fireman Parks caught the attention of Lieutenant Gerard and he made the long arduous trek to the crest of Beaver Snatch where he encountered a group of gathering fire fighters standing in awe of the sight before their eyes.

Making his way around the tight group he was heard to exclaim, "Well I'll be dammed! What the hell?"

CONTENTS

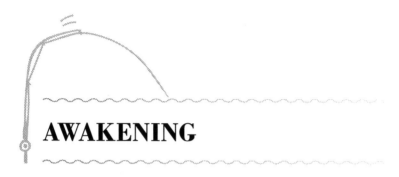

AWAKENING

Early morning light danced and dappled the walls of the modest front bedroom of an older house at 16607 Salem Ave. in northwest Detroit. The gently swaying curtains created a warming design that washed over the fading wallpaper.

There was a subdued squeak of a cry.

He wasn't. He was.

No different than virtually every other child born.

Charles (Charlie) Garnet Knordfnerk arrived at a modest family in a modest home in the postwar forties. He joined the bow wave of a generation to be known as the baby boomers.

Charlie's mother, Gertrude O'Dell Knordfnerk and father, Ebenezer Garnet Knordfnerk, had planned for more than one child and certainly closer together but a depression and war had interceded. Thus, William Knordfnerk had celebrated his tenth birthday only two days before and was hardly enamored with the thought of sharing his life with a little brother. William and his buddies swore an oath never to have anything to do with their siblings and to his credit Paul was good to his word.

Charlie would have to be his last hurrah, as Neezer saw it, as war wounds prevented more gainful employment and the probability of having another child would take a miracle.

Gertrude was grateful Charlie didn't look like his father.

The Sunday of Charlie's baptism witnessed the gathering of the Knordfnerk Clan and the O'Dell mob. For the most part they were civil and polite though Neezer's brother Bravin felt it his duty to challenge any and all O'Dell's to hand-to-hand combat. Seventeen beers usually did that to him.

Gertrude's Sister Patricia O'Dell, not being the center of the world on this day, proceeded to entertain anyone within earshot of her disease of the month. Any prior acquaintances knew to steer clear. If there had been an international organization of "The Decease of the Month Club" she would surely been President Emeritus.

Willi and Peter O'Dell found entertainment behind the garage with young Babel Knordfnerk. It seemed she had a new kind of tobacco and the three experimenters wafted off to OZ. Babel never could understand how she ended up wearing Willis's underwear over top of her slacks. Pete was incoherent for three days.

Young William discovered a new game with his cousin Peggy called stinky finger. Young explorers seem to be the same the world over.

The festivities winding down as they were Gertrude decided to remove Charlie's baptismal gown and preserve it for the next one in the family to need it. The gown had been in the family over 180 years and had deposits from neigh onto 100 ancestors.

Charlie lay on the bed in his altogether for all to admire. Patricia made the rude comment that Charlie hardly came close to her son for good looks. She did however admire his oversized pickle and thought some young lady might find it passable in twenty years or so.

As the idle chatter ensued Charlie did as many a lad had done before. Charlie raised his pickle and let fly a stream to make any beer drinker proud. His aim not being what would be desired the stream found its mark directly in his own face. Just in time to witness the second christening of the day Uncle Bravin in his inimitable way punctuated the event. "Welcome to life Charlie".

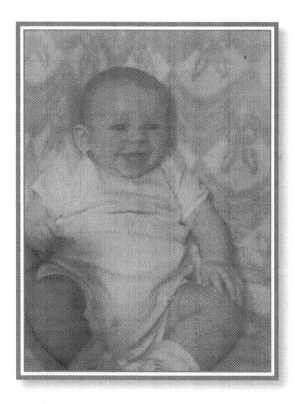

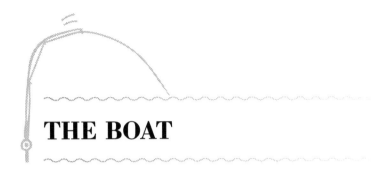

THE BOAT

C harlie and his best bud Paul, fishing poles in hand followed a well-worn trail to their favorite fishing hole. The early air was cool and damp making it the perfect time to catch more than enough grasshoppers for bait as their spring legs were too cold to work. The trail split with the two anglers taking the little used barely noticeable trail to the left.

The right trail was reserved for teens use only. Friday and Saturday initiation into adulthood rituals was sacred ground in these parts.

As the boys picked their way into a clearing a black cat leapt out of the weeds in pursuit of a vole. Paul, startled, fell back into the grass. Charlie never blinked an eye. Being a sage observer of life, he stood and watched as the critters disappeared into the weeds on the opposite side of the path.

"My brother sure is weird," Charlie stated, "He says he eats those things over yonder. (Indicating the path to the right) I never could eat a pussycat." Paul simply stared at Charlie; a questioning look on his face. Shaking off the leaves and weeds Paul snatched his pole from the thatch and caught up to Charlie and they proceeded to the fishing hole.

From time-to-time things floated by their perch. They usually used those occasions to practice their accuracy in casting at a moving target. Today provided an especially unique target. An empty boat presented itself near the center of the river, an inviting target. Casts were sent out again and again with no success. Just as the boat was about out of range Charlie hooked it on the end and started reeling it in. Fighting the current of the river Charlie was able to coax the boat ashore about one hundred feet from their perch. As Charlie steadied the boat Paul ran down with stringer in hand and secured it to a tree jutting out into the river.

This was one fine boat, room for both and all their tackle. It was comfortable and pretty with no markings, names or numbers on the sides.

"We got us a fishin boat Paul and we are going to catch every fish in this river now."

"Don't you think we should tell someone about this boat Charlie?"

"Heck no, they would just take it away from us and besides their ain't no name on it so finders' keepers."

Paul, a dubious look on his face shrugged his shoulders submitted. "Ok Charlie but if we get in trouble, it's your fault."

"We won't get in trouble and besides no one used a boat here, just canoes."

And so, commenced the summer of the boat. Day after day the boys were able to get into areas they had never been before, and the fishing was great. Canoeists were noisy so it was easy for the twosome to evade them. Why you could hear them twenty minutes before they appeared. Every evening they would pull their yacht into a back cove where none ever came.

June turned into July and July turned into August. The new school year was fast approaching, and the boys started wondering what they were going to do with their boat. They couldn't just leave it in the river, it would sink for sure. They had nearly lost it once from a three-day rain and didn't want to tempt fate again.

"Let's take it to your place Paul, your dad will never notice it behind the garage."

"No way, my dad finds it and I'm going to get killed. You caught it, it's yours, you take it home."

"You are closer, we can get to your house without anyone noticing. My house is too far."

The bickering lasted about one week when the decision was taken away from them. A state game warden checking on the fish population spotted the boys. They were able to evade him but the next day he brought a posse, and the jig was up. Three game wardens and two township police cornered the boys just as they were about to launch into a new day of fishing. The boat was confiscated, and the boys taken to the police station.

"You boys are in a heap of trouble. Probably get twenty years in prison for stealing that thing." Captain Greer had the boys close to tears on the trip to the station. "You got some tall explaining to do. The judge isn't going to go lightly on you two"

When they arrived Charlie's and Paul's parents were already there. They were escorted into a room and given the third degree. "Where did you boys steal that thing from?" "When did you get that thing?" "Why didn't you boys report this to the police?"

About twenty minutes into the interrogation an elderly man

entered the room. "I think I can fill in some of the questions officer. That was the Evers coffin. It washed out of the cemetery this spring during that heavy rain in April. We figured it had sunk and never found any remains.

"What's a coffin?" Charlie had never heard a boat called that before.

"That's what we bury dead people in Charlie, your boat was what old Mrs. Evers was buried in last year."

No wonder their boat had been so plush. Too bad, that was the best boat they had ever seen. Oh well, school would take their minds off the loss of the yacht soon.

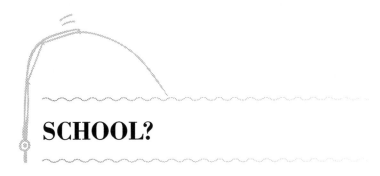

SCHOOL?

A new classroom. A new teacher. Same ol kids from last year. Yost Elementary would never change.

Two new kids showed up the second day. Wow! Twins! Wow! The teacher wrote their names on the blackboard, Evonne and Evette. Nice names, pretty girls. They get to sit in the empty seats on either side of Charlie. Charlie couldn't look up at them for the first week. Massive shyness took over and massive kidding from his bud Paul. "Charlie has two girlfriends. Charlie has two girlfriends". Paul teased him all weekend.

But the second week got worse. Mrs. Nobble, the new second grade teacher assigned the students to groups to work on a project to be completed by the end of the year. The project? How to write a book. What the heck, he could hardly read, how could he write a book? His partners? Evonne and Evette!

Paul had a field day. All weekend he teased until Charlie went home early Sunday and refused to eat his supper. William gladly finished it for him.

Slumped in his chair he refused to look up as Evonne and Evette approached their seats. They both stopped and placed a small package on Charlies desk before sitting on theirs. What was this? A bribe? Cookies? What a dastardly act! They did look good! They did taste good! Wow, great girls! And they were all Charlies!

After recess the teacher had the students break up into their groups. All were groups of four but Charlie, Evonne and Evette. Mrs. Nobble explained that writing a book was easy but hard. The hard part was thinking up what to write about. The easy part was writing. She explained you write what you like to do so it becomes easy and fun. If it is fun for someone else, they like to read it. If it is also a subject, they like they also would like to write about it as well. So first off you have to talk together about what you like to do and come up with a subject for your story. You may not decide today but work on it and don't you all just talk. There is no bossing anyone here, only compromising. What a bummer, two girls, what on earth could they ever have in common to write about? Play with dolls? Bake cookies? Dress up their dog? Braid their hair? Have tea parties?

They started to compare notes. After an hour they had nothing when Mrs. Nobble suggested they compare notes on what they did last summer. Ok, play with dolls, no! Braid their hair, no! Dress their dog? NO! Go fishing? Wait, did they say go fishing? YES!!!

That was the magic word! They started talking and talking about fishing till the bell rang and they had to go home. Or did they? On the way home the girls had to pass Charlie's house, so they stopped on the front porch and talked and talked some more. At 5:00 a lady came walking down the street and called out to Evonne and Evette. Their Mom! Boy, were they going to be in trouble now! Charlie's Mom came out to see what the problem and the mothers stood and listened to the children tell their mothers what was going on. They both just stood and listened as the kids got excited telling everything till the girls mom went inside with Charlie's mom to have a cup of tea and get acquainted.

7:00 P.M. came around and the girl's father showed up to take them and their mother home in their car. WHAT A DAY! Charlie fell in love with both and decided he would marry one or both of them!

For the first time in his school career Charlie actually did homework. He wrote everything he could think about fishing for the book.

Thursday morning, he waited for the girls, and they walked to school together talking all the way about fishing.

The afternoon class came, and the groups got together and the three got a blazing start but soon ran into a roadblock. How do you start a book?

Mrs. Nobble to the rescue! She called the class to attention and helped them start an outline on starting their books. First the subject. Second an outline on how you would present the subject. Third what you like about the subject in each section. Fourth, start writing each section of the outline.

Next go back and go over every section together until you agree you all like it and no bullies. Next rewrite the book. Next go over it again and if you like it present it to the teacher for assessment. Next make any corrections suggestions made by the teacher and present it to the class. Minimum of twenty pages and maximum of 30 pages. Two months to complete. This was to be half the English grade for the year.

The trio took off like ducks to water. They met almost every day after school till late May. Fr some unknown reason the girls missed school for a week. Then a second week and a third. Charlie got very worried and talked with his mom about it and she informed him the girls were very sick.

Charlie went to the girls house after school the next day and their mom told him the girls would not be able to come to school for the rest of the year. He asked if he could see them and was politely told that would be impossible. Despondent Charlie went home and asked his mom what was wrong, and she told him the girls had Polio. "What's Polio"? Charlie quarried. "It's a disease some people get that makes it impossible to walk and they have to stay in a machine for about a year to help them breath.

Charlie was devastated. He had finally met not one but two girls worth liking and now they were taken away from him. What would happen to their book?

The next day at school Charlie approached Mrs. Nobble and told her about the problem. She suggested he join another group, but he was adamant about finishing their book with them some way. They talked about it during recess and during afternoon class.

After school Charlie started writing an outline of the problem and how to fix it. He presented it to Mrs. Nobble the next day and it impressed her very much. She presented it to the principle for his input and he was all in.

To Charlies surprise his mother walked with him to school and they went to the principal's office where the girls mother was waiting. They sat down and the principle asked Charlie what he had in mind.

Charlie got up and slowly started, "Mrs. Nobble told us to write a book and she showed us how to get started when we had a problem getting started, Evonne, Evette and I had a problem till we found we all love to fish, and it was magic. We got started and couldn't stop. Now they are sick, and we need to finish the book so I thought it was like a problem so I wrote an outline on how we could still finish our book together. I still have two good legs so I can take what we come up with to their house for their mom to read to them. They can tell their mom what they want to write and what they think about what I write and every day I can take it to school for a little help from Mrs. Nobble. I already started and I know that it won't be easy for the girls so I will do what they can't.

The principle looked at all in attendance with a questioning look in his eye and asked, "Well, any thoughts."

The girls mother was stunned as was Charlies. Mrs. Nobble was all smiles. Charlie blushed but didn't say anything.

"If it's ok with everyone I think this is a wonderful idea and we should let Charles go ahead with it." The principle stated.

"This is too much to ask of Charlie." The girl's mother stated.

"I agree", said Charlie's mother.

"I don't, they are my friends, I want to do it for them." Charlie stood up with an air of authority and a look of determination on his face.

"That settles it, Charlie, you have a green light, go ahead."

"Why do I have a green light?"

The laughter released any tension in the room.

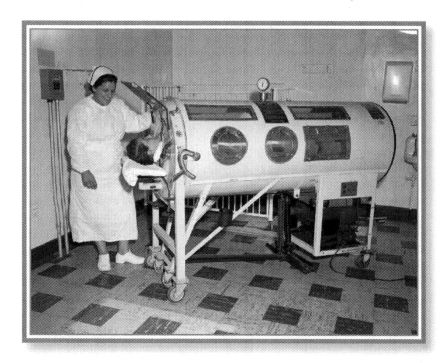

So, Charlie took on the job. Writing. Taking what he wrote to the girls mother so she could read it to them. Getting their feedback from their mother and rewriting. Going to class and working with Mrs. Nobble and repeating the same routine for over a month till they all agreed it was done.

Two weeks before the end of the semester the book was turned in to Mrs. Nobble. It was placed on the stack of all the books from all the teams. From his seat it didn't look any different than any other books, but Charlie knew which one was his and the girls. he was relieved it was done. Now he could look forward to the summer vacation and fishing.

The last day of school arrived, and Charlie was surprised his mother walked to school with him. When they arrived, he was even more surprised to see his dad waiting for them. They went into the

Gym and all the kids from the school were seated along with all the teachers. What was going on?

Nine chairs were in front of the room with a microphone set up. The Principle, Mrs. Nobble and two other men were seated waiting for someone. When Charlie, his mom and dad were directed to take seats Charlie was somewhat confused. Then The girls mother and father came in and sat in the last two seats along.

The principal got up and called for the kids to come to order and Pledge Allegiance to the Flag. Everyone got up, faced the flag and together recited "I pledge allegiance to the flag of the United States of America and to the Republic for which it stands. One Nation, indivisible, with liberty and justice for all." When they all had returned to their seats, he called everyone's attention to the next speaker.

Charlies teacher Mrs. Nobble. She approached the podium and started telling everyone how all the students had a project to write a book as their class project. There was no failing but the better the groups did the better grade they got. She explained how the groups were set up with four students in each group keeping the groups evenly split between boys and girls. There was one group left with only three kids made up of two girls and one boy. Each group got to pick the topic of their book and they had two months to complete. All the groups did a very god job, but one group had to go above and beyond to complete their task. That brings us to giving recognition to that group today. You only see one of the groups here today and that is because the other two members, Evonne and Evette McCloud came down with Polio and have not been able to attend school for three months. Charles Knordfnerk, the third member was the legs of this group and between the three they accomplished quite a task indeed. I would like to call Mrs. Knordfnerk up to tell us how this started.

Charlies mom came forward and looking back at her son started. "I could never have imagined Charlie doing what he did. He had always been a shy boy and other than fishing from an abandoned coffin never got into any trouble. When he came home with the two girls after school one day the three sat on the front porch and carried on an excited conversation for over an hour till the girl's mother showed up looking for her daughters. She didn't want to disturb them, so we went in for some tea and the chance to get acquainted. She called her husband to come and pick them up when he came home from work. We sat where we could hear the kids and were enchanted by their enthusiasm. They just talked about fishing and how much fun they had last summer vacation doing more fishing than ever before. When their father came to pick them up Mrs. McCloud and I agreed to get together again and encourage the kids in their task. I will turn it over to Mrs. McCloud to go on from here."

Mrs. McCloud came to the microphone and smiling started. "I am very happy my girls met Charlie and his mother. We have all become very good friends. After they met, my girls couldn't stop talking about Charly and how he loved fishing just like they did. When they started writing their book Mrs. Nobble gave them the means to proceed and they took off like a jet. They were doing great until my girls got sick and couldn't go to school. It was two weeks before we knew it was polio and we were devastated. The girls were heartbroken, not because they were sick but because they couldn't finish their book with Charlie. The third week we received two iron lungs for them to help them breath and a short time later Charlie

15

came to see the girls, but I had to tell him he couldn't, they were sick with polio. He left sad faced and walking slow. I will turn it over to Mrs. Nobble from here."

Mrs. Nobble came back to the microphone. "Charlie came to perplexed about the book he and the girls were writing. I suggested he join another group. "No Maam, this is the girls book, and I can't let them down just because they are sick. There must be some way we can finish it." To which I said that may not be possible but if you can come up with an idea, I will be happy to hear it. He went home that day promising to come back tomorrow with his idea. Sure enough he did, and this is what he did. He would be the legs for the girls and write what they wanted and add some of his ideas. Take it back to them and go back and forth until the book was finished. It had to be okey with all parties, so I asked for a meeting with the principle, Mrs. Knordfnerk and Mrs. McCloud. We met with Charlie and talked it over and Charlie won the day. The book they produced was more than good, it made me believe in the goodness of young people going above and beyond for their friends. I will turn it over to our principle for the rest of the story."

The principle came back to the microphone and asked Charlie to come up with him. "I want to introduce you all to Charlie!" He stood back and applauded Charlie as well as everyone in the room. "Charlie, when we met the day you took on this job, I didn't know how it would turn out. I did know you had your mind set and knowing it would be a very tough job I had my doubts, but you came through and the three of you accomplished a task above and beyond your years. Evonne and Evette can't be here today but we are recording this so they can hear everything. We also have something special for the three of you. From the Detroit News writer Jerome Mimes is here to tell us just what it is. Mr. Mimes."

Mr. Mimes came to the microphone. "This is an honor to be here and meet young Mr. Knordfnerk and hear about this story. I am very touched and proud of you Charlie as well as Evette and Evonne. It isn't very often we hear a story about young people developing such a strong friendship and loyalty that extends to this level. After I heard about this from your Principle, I approached our editor with a request. Not only to honor the three of you for your work but to have your book entered into a young authors library at the Detroit News. It is available at the Detroit News offices for anyone to read. We honor you!"

With that the audience stood and started clapping very loud. The principle waved his hands to stop the clapping and when it got quiet, he asked Charlie, "Well Charlie, what do you want to do this summer now that this school year is done?"

"Go fishing!"

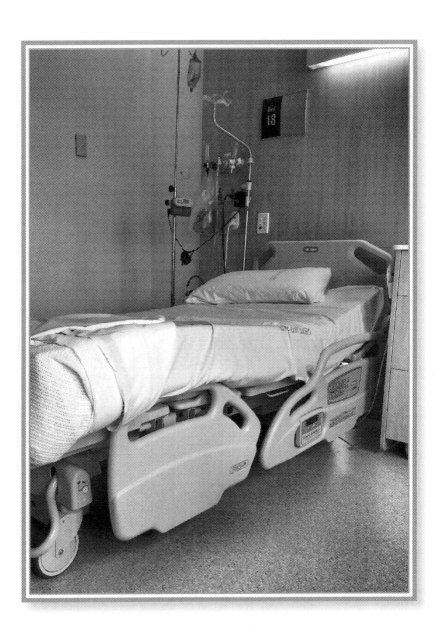

THE BIG SICK

The new school year started before Charlie knew what happened. Evonne and Evette had moved away to be near other family, so his closest friends were gone. Only Paul remained but it wasn't the same. They fished and caught plenty but without the boat that was all they had in common.

So school, new teachers, mostly the same kids. Nine months to go before freedom to fish every day.

September came and went. October pretty much the same.

November started pretty much the same but the second week something was wrong. Charlie got sick. It wasn't the usual kid sick it was different. After a week Charlie got very weak. His legs started aching and he could hardly walk.

His father took Charlie to the Doctors office, and he took blood samples and sent Charlie back home. The next day the doctor called and told Charlies mother to take Charlie to Detroit Osteopathic Hospital right away. She called a cab and took Charlie to the hospital where he was admitted and started treatment for Rheumatic Fever. Later the doctor came to see Charlie and his mother.

"I wish we had caught this earlier, but it is what it is. Charlie has a severe case of Rheumatic Fever which attacks the heart and outer limbs. He will regain his legs in time, but he may have heart damage. We won't know for a while about that. He may be here for some time."

Some time turned from a week to two to three to a month before Charlie was able to go home. During that time Charlie fell in love with a pretty young nurse named Rebecca who tended to Charlie every day when she was on duty and even visited him when she had a day off. She reminded Charlie of the twins she even knew about the book they had written. She was glad he was going home but he had mixed feelings.

When he arrived home the house was rearranged. A bedroom had been set up in the dining room since he couldn't walk and going up stairs every day several times would be hard on his mother. He couldn't walk so he dragged himself around the house. It took three months to regain his ability to walk but on the bright side he was free from school, or so he thought.

A tutor started coming once a week till Charlie could stand more. Then a second day, then a third. When he became comfortable with that the hours were stretched to about four a day. Which was about all he could take. He finished the school year but with only half a year's credit.

When he was able to walk, he started exploring his back yard. Then his front yard, then his street.

He met new people, but they all seemed to know him already.

There was one lady he absolutely didn't like. Mrs. Rutherford. A mean old lady who always yelled at the kids as they walked past her house on their way to and from school. She even called the school to report Charlie had stolen flowers from her garden after she had given them to him to give to his teacher. His mother gave him a spanking for that before she found the truth.

Charlie held a grudge, and he was determined to get even. In July his opportunity presented itself. Wandering along the street on trash pickup day he examined many offerings put out at the curb by his neighbors and glory be he found something that might work. It was a jar of something that smelled bad. It just might do the trick.

That evening just before he had to go home, he sneaked behind Mrs. Rutherford's house and spread the stuff on the outside of her rear door. It was enough to cover a good area. He promptly went home.

The next day was a proper hot July day and the cure worked. The area around Mrs. Rutherford's house really smelled bad but it was so bad she couldn't open her windows. She came out yelling at everyone accusing anyone she saw of doing something to her house. She called the police and when they came, they said there was nothing they could do but warned her to stop making so much noise or her neighbors might file a complaint against her.

Several neighbors got together and cleaned the back of her house only after she promised to stop bothering all the kids walking by her house. She agreed and the neighborhood settled down.

Charlies father asked him what it was on her house and without thinking he dug the empty container and gave it to him. He immediately burst into laughter the likes of which Charlie had never heard before or since. The laughter was heard around the neighborhood as Charlies father toured with container in hand telling everyone he met what had caused such a ruckus. Charlies esteem grew in his neighbors eyes after that.

As the new school year approached Charlie was able to steer out of most trouble. He did have to go to summer school for two months in the mornings which messed much of the best fishing time.

NEW SCHOOL YEAR,
NEW TROUBLES

C harlie was able to go to two extra hours every day and stay with his classmates which made him happy but left him with little time for himself in the afternoon. He made up for it by learning how to tie fly fishing lures but had no idea how he would use them. Maybe he would learn how to learn how to fly fish next summer.

Paul and Charlie slipped back into their old groove on Saturdays and made up for the missed days with a skipped afternoon once in a while to check out the river and make sure everything was alright.

On their second recon mission they found something that got them scared and they returned to school to report it to the principal. He quickly called the police who came to the school to interview the kids.

When they finished talking to the two, they asked the principal to call the kids parents and ask permission to have the kids lead the police to what they found to confirm what they suspected.

Ten minutes later they were seated in the back of the police car traveling to the location.

Arriving the four got out of the car and Charlie and Paul led the police to the burnt spot. On closer examination they could see dozens of burnt hypodermic needles and bottles that indicated morphine. One officer got a camera out of the police car and started taking pictures. The second officer called the station and informed his sergeant what they found. He came back with a small shovel and bag but instead of digging told his partner investigators were on their way and they were to wait there.

At that time a man from across the street approached them and asked what they were doing?

"These young lads found this and brought us here to check it out."

"That must be from Nurse Adams from next door. She often brings stuff home after her duty at the hospital and burns it here."

"Thanks, we will take care of it. You have to leave now; our investigators are on the way."

He left and not three minutes later two more police cars came and parked.

One of the officers not dressed in police cloths came up to Paul first then Charlie and introduced himself as Lt. Schaefer.

"I understand you fellows found this stuff here and reported it to your school, is that right?"

They both nodded agreements.

"Tell me what you were doing out of school at that time?"

Charlie shrugged, "Skipping I guess."

"Where you supposed to be in school?"

"Yes sir."

"Well, I am glad you reported what you found here but it would be better if you stayed in school. Someone could have seen you here

24

and come and hurt you very bad. That would not have been good for you, would it?"

"No sir, we are sorry."

"Lieutenant Schaefer, I think you need to see this." One of the police called who had been wandering around the area.

Lieutenant Schaefer went to where the other policeman was and stared at an object on the ground. "Call in for forensics and backup. This is more than it first looked like. Also take the kids back to school asap." Charlie and Paul were whisked off to school before they could blink. Their parents were waiting for them, they both received the third degree at school, on the way home and again at home.

Charlie was grounded for two weeks.

Their names were left out, but the story made the front page of the Detroit News and Detroit Free Press. It also led to a murder conviction and drug convictions.

So went the highlight of another schoolyear.

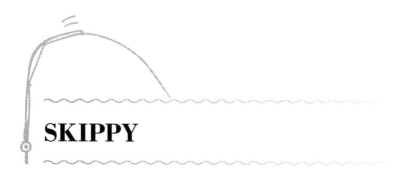

SKIPPY

S pring came with promise of some freedom. Charlie got around but again had a tutor teach him every day to try and keep him up on his classes. The boys were not allowed to see each other because of all the trouble they caused, and Charlie was never allowed to go to the river. His only fishing time was with his father at Anchor Bay for an afternoon fishing off a dock with no results. He couldn't even go to nearby parks to fish. What a bummer.

School came too soon and the same as usual. At least he and Paul were able to get back together but it was at a new school and new teachers. Houghton was bigger than his first school, more grades and a lot more kids. It was a lot further and Charlie had to take a bus to school for the first time. It only took ten minutes to take the bus to school, but he missed the five-minute walk from the last years. There were too many kids, he would have to remember so many names and new teachers to remember as well. He also was surprised to learn he would have five teachers every day! Yikes! Who was the crazy person who thought this crazy idea up?

So, it started. The first week Charlie got lost going from one class twice to his embarrassment. The second week only once. The big kids loved to bully the new little kids which included Charlie who was much smaller than most boys his age. This was not going to be a fun year of school.

Luckily Charlie finished September. November didn't go as well. Around the middle of the month something familiar came visiting. He was getting sick again and this time his father took him to the doctor's office right away. Sure enough, he had Rheumatic Fever again!

He went to the hospital again, but this time only spent two weeks as they had new treatments which got him back home much quicker.

He still couldn't walk when he got home but his arms were stronger, and he was able to get around better. He got a very strong shot of bycillin every week and after three weeks was able to start walking. He was able to go to the back yard where he was visited by a new acquaintance. A black long-haired dog named Skippy. They became friends quickly as Charly was the only kid around during the day. Charlie tied his wagon to Skippy's collar and the two of them explored the area for hours until the snow came. When it cleared, Skippy would come to the back door and scratch on it till Charlie came out. Charlie started teaching Skippy tricks which he loved. Fetch was easy. Finding hidden things was a little harder but quickly learned. Even finding things hidden in the fallen leaves was no challenge. Leaping in the air to catch the ball was quick. Jumping over the picnic table was more of a challenge, but after a day he became adept. Leaping a fence also took a day. Skippy could do anything!

After New Year Skippy quickly learned to pull Charlie around on his new sled. This opened up new vistas to exploration. The golf course two blocks away was a mecca the two loved. Charlie sliding downhill, Skippy running along beside. Finally, Skippy learned to ride the sled down the hill and pull it up. These were glorious times for them both.

As the snow disappeared and the mud became the terrain of the day they travelled less often. Skippy would disappear for long stretches of time until April when trouble came along. It seemed there were a large number of puppies that were being born in the neighborhood. It also was strange that they were almost all black. It also seemed the puppies started to appear about two months after Skippy learned to jump over fences. What a coincidence!

Charlie's parents got several calls about their dog. They were curious as to why everyone thought they had a dog. Asking Charlie about it he admitted teaching Skippy tricks and how Skippy pulled him around the neighborhood. When asked where Skippy came from, he simply answered, "God sent him!"

There were quite a few angry people around the neighborhood. Most wanted Skippy put down. Many wanted him sent to the Humane Society. No one knew where he came from or who he belonged to. Finally, an elderly neighbor, Mr. Adams, said he would adopt Skippy and have him fixed. He was lonely and Skippy would be the perfect companion. That settled it. At least Charlie could see Skippy every day and they could still be best buddies.

Summer would soon be here, and other kids would be available to play with. Maybe someone might even like fishing?

OPEN AIR SCHOOL!

Charlie was finally allowed to go back to school. The school he was to attend was Edgar A. Guest School. This was a coincidence as his grandfather on his mother's side, Ebenezer was a friend of Mr. Guest. Mr. Guest was a poet who Charlie had met when at his grandfather's house when he was about five years old. Mr. Guest was visiting his grandfather as well and they were all sitting down for Sunday dinner. As the meal was progressing Mr. Guest tapped Charlie on the Shoulder and asked, "Be a stepper and pass the pepper please!" Charlie had no idea what he meant but everyone else laughed. Charlies mother came to his rescue and handed him the pepper to pass to Mr. Guest.

That was about as close as Charlie would come to a famous person, but it didn't make much difference to Charlie. It was just a name.

Besides being named after a former Poet Laureate of Michigan what good was the school? Charlie was stuck in what was called the "Open air room," which meant all the kids with handicaps. Charlie couldn't run but he could walk. Charlie could read.

Charlie had all his faculties. What was he doing in the "Open Air Room"?

When he went home Charlie told his mother what his day was like. He was very upset. There was no teaching. There was only someone that watched all the kids to make sure they didn't hurt themselves. He didn't want to go back to school, he only wanted to stay home and play with Skippy. His mother would hear nothing of the kind. She would go with Charlie the next day and get everything straightened out.

Sure thing, the next morning Charlies mother got on the bus with Charlie, and they had the quietest ride to school in recorded history. On arrival they went to the principals office to get permission for her to visit Charlies class. Entering the classroom, the attendant came up to Charlies mother and told her she was not allowed there. Mrs. Knordfnerk handed a slip of paper to the young lady who promptly left for the principals office. Charlies mom sat in a chair and watched the kids who wandered aimlessly around making noises and never sat in their chairs.

After five minutes the attendant and the principal came into the room and asked Mrs. Knordfnerk what she wanted? She looked up at them and handed them a sheet of paper. After reading the paper the principle turned red and started apologizing for the mistake that had been made. He quickly escorted them out of the room and to the principles office. The principle got on the phone and talked with someone for about ten minutes in a room adjacent to his office and when finished came back to his office.

"Mrs. Knordfnerk, Charlie, I am very sorry for the mistake and discomfort you had to endure. Someone higher up determined you having been sick so much the last two years must have been very handicapped but evidently you are not. I humbly apologize. You should not have even been sent to this school; the school you should have been sent to is Hubert which is much closer to your home. I have straightened out everything for you and again I am very sorry for this incident. After I read what Charlie did for the twins and that accolades, he received I know he is an outstanding young man, and you must be proud of him."

Charlies mother stood up and thanked the principle, motioned for Charlie to get up and they exited the school.

It was a short walk to where they caught the city bus that would take them to another bus that would take them to Salem Street and home.

So went his short stay at the school named after his grandfather's friend.

MIDDLE SCHOOL

W ow, this was really different! This school was big! Two floors! There must have been twenty busses lined up with kids getting out and more coming as the ones now empty left.

Hubert Middle School sure was a lot better than what Charlie had been used to. Almost everyone was new! Only the kids from Charlies bus were familiar. It was a little scarry but thrilling too. Everyone had to go to the auditorium first to meet their teachers for their hour. First hour? What was that?

Entering the auditorium, the kids were directed to different areas according to their grade. 7A or 7B, 8A or 8B, 9A or 9B. The older kids acted like it was old hat. They joked around and made fun of the baby 7A's. this was unsettling, they had been the big kids just a short time ago now they were the babies? Charlie would have to write to the Governor of something, this wasn't right. It was unfair.

They were introduced to Mr. Wallace. What was this? A man teacher? That can't be. There must be a mistake.

He led them to a room on the second floor. Number 213 to be exact. On the blackboard was written their schedule for every day. Hour #1, room 213. Subject, English. Hour #2, room 226. Subject, History. Hour #3, Subject, Math, room 216. Lunch. Hour #4, subject Social Studies, room 213 again. Hour #5, subject, Gym, room Gymnasium. End of day 3:00 P.M.

How was Charlie supposed to keep all of this in his head? Also, each student had an assigned seat. Charlie found himself seated in a familiar place, the back row. He even had a girl sitting next to him. Maybe she could even fish? He would have to ask.

Mr. Wallace called everyone to attention. "I want everyone to write down the schedule you see on the board. Next, I want you to write down your reading assignment for tonight, chapter 1 of the textbook you will be taking home with you. Don't forget to bring it back with you tomorrow." He started writing on the board, "An Empty Mind is an Empty Life. The Way to a Full Mind and Life is Through Reading." He turned to the class and asked. "Can anyone tell me what this means? No one raised their hands. "I am going to call on someone who should know. Charlie Knordfnerk, what do you think it means"? at Charlies name several kids laughed. "No laughing at peoples names allowed in this room or you will spend the hour standing in the front corner. Charlie what do you think?"

Charlie started to say something. "Please stand Mr. Knordfnerk."

Charlie stood up; red faced at being the first one called up for anything in the class. "I think if you want to learn about the world or anything else the best way is to read about it."

"I couldn't have said it any better Mr. Knordfnerk. I understand you had quite a bit of time to read and even write is that correct?"

"Yes sir."

"I am not making Charles a target for any of you, on the contrary,

I know he is a person who will go out of his way to help any of you having trouble reading. Is that right Charles?"

"Yes sir, I love to read and write."

"Great, you all heard that. So, you have two teachers in this class now and we can all be thankful for that. Now turn to the first chapter and we will get started."

So went the first hour.

Hour two, History. This was Charlies favorite subject. He didn't know why but he loved reading about things that happened in the past and who had done what. The teacher was Mrs. Clarke. A middle-aged woman with a passion for teaching. She outlined what they would be learning for the semester and the reading assignment for the first week. This class went quite fast and before he knew it he was headed to the third hour class, Math.

This math was different, Miss Abigale was the teacher and algebra was the new kind of math they would be learning. As it turned out it wasn't new at all. It was created by the Arabs or a close group of people to them over two thousand years ago. It was supposed to make math easier but the first day did anything but do that. Time would tell. After math was lunch hour. Here they went to a lunchroom where you could get a hot or cold lunch or bring your own lunch in a bag or lunch box. Charlie joined a bunch of his classmates sitting at a table with home made lunches.

They were pretty quiet, unlike the other kids in the lunchroom. There was a lot of laughing, yelling, food throwing and teasing of other kids. As might be expected attention turned to their table and the one next to them, the rest of their grade.

"Hay babies, how do you like big kids school?"

"You are going to hate it here when we get done with you!"

"Let us have your lunch!" One big yelled as he came toward their tables and grabbed a sandwich from a girl in Charlies class.

"Hey, Harvey, do they have anything any good?" Another boy yelled as he approached. "Nope none here!" he yelled as he grabbed something from another kids lunch bag and threw it at Harvey. This started a food fight with other kids form other tabled coming to the "Babies" table, grabbing any food they could and throwing it at the kids sitting in dismay, crying and ducking as best they could.

At that point the lunchroom monitor, Mr. Bemis, the Gym teacher came up, grabbed a couple of the bullies and yelled stopping the remnants of the meylay.

"What the Hell do you think you are doing? All of you brain dead bullies come with me!"

He lined up six of seven of the culprits, missing Harvey, and marched them down to the principal's office.

The bell rang and the everyone left the room except the babies who were directed to stay. The lunch staff came out and gave them all ice-cream cones which helped settle them down and they went on to their next class, Social Studies about ten minutes late.

Charlie thought Social Studies would be the same as history, but it wasn't. the teacher, Mrs. Swaith, corrected the misconception right away.

"In History you will be learning about a single country usually, such as the American History. In Social Studies you will be learning about the why and wherefore of the development of politics, laws, relationships between countries, and much more. We will learn how and why we became a nation. How and why the Constitution was written. How and why new states joined and much much more. We will only scratch the surface of the subject here. It will take you a lifetime to learn it all if that were even possible."

The class was shortened but filled with things Charlie found interesting and was looking forward to learning more about Social Studies.

Time for fifth hour and Mr. Bemis. The kids thought he would be a nice man and take care of them after what had happened in the lunchroom. Boy were they wrong!

Mr. Bemis yelled out. Boys line up on my right and girls on my left."

As might be expected some of the kids got their right and left wrong which became clear quickly.

"You really are babies, aren't you? My right is your left, got that? My left is your right, got that?"

Now the kids got it straight. They were too scared to get it wrong.

"I want to see who is faster, the boys of the girls. When I blow my whistle, the boys will start running to the far end of the Gym and back one at a time one after each other until you are all are done. At the same time the girls will start running to the far end and back one at a time until you are all are done. Does everyone understand?"

Everyone nodded.

"Now, from the front first when you hear the whistle go!"

Mr. Bemis blew the whistle and the first two took off. It was close until the fourth kids. The boy, Freddy, was very chubby and slow. He barely made it back and the girl next up was halfway to the back of the gym. The next six kids couldn't make a dent in the girls lead. Charlie was the anchor, and he was determined to catch up.

When he started the gap was quite large, but the last girl was not fast. She was having trouble running and it would be easy for Charlie to beat her. Touching the back wall Charlie was only about ten feet behind her and would pass her in twenty feet easily. As he neared her something clicked in his brain. It would not be right to beat someone having trouble running. He had been there himself. When he came even with her, he held out his hand and she looked at him wondering what was wrong with him.

"Come on, we all win here."

She reached out her hand and they both crossed the finish line together.

The other kids were stunned.

Mr. Bemis was stunned.

Only Charlie and his new friend were not. She gave him a big hug and smiled brighter than she had in quite a while.

"This is a lesson I guess we needed to learn after lunch today. Teamwork is the best way for all of us to get along in this world and to protect ourselves against bullies. Thank you, Mr. Knordfnerk, well done!"

With that all the kids gathered around the two finalists and everyone slapped their backs.

The rest of fifth hour went as might be expected and the first day of middle school ended.

On to the busses and home.

"How was school today, Charles?" asked his mother.

"Ok, nothing special. Just a bunch of new kids and a bunch of big kids too."

Charlie did well enough in seventh grade. His classmates liked him, he liked them. They still had trouble with bullies though and Charlie became the class champion defending his mates. He got his butt kicked more often than not but he got his licks in too. Some of the other boys in his class started backing him up and by the end of the year no one tried to intimidate the babies anymore.

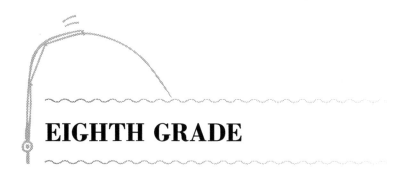

EIGHTH GRADE

A new day, a new grade, new friends.

As the first day of the new school started the new babies were huddled at the 7A tables as usual. The kids from the 7B table came over and started teasing them as this was their first time as bigger kids. Charlie walked up with a couple of other 8A boys and introduced themselves to the new 7A kids and informed them there would not be any trouble from any upper grades or whoever gave them trouble would answer to the 8A Team.

The 7B bullies quietly went back to their tables and no word came from the upper-class tables. From then on, the die was set and the 8A oversaw all incoming classes and protected them from upper class bullies and no further trouble ever occurred.

Charlie was enamored with his new classes and looked forward to meeting a lot of new kids. These kids came from a large area of Detroit. Many from several miles from where he lived on the northwest corner of the city. The mix of kids was different too. For the first time some of the kids he went to school with were black.

Some kids made fun of them, and he didn't know why so he asked one black boy in his class why other kids made fun of him?

"Are you kidding man?"

"No, you are the first black boy I have met, and I don't know why the other kids make fun of you. I'm Charlie."

"Well, you got some learned to do. I'm Derick, I can teach you, but it would be better if my mamma did. Come with me after school and she can set you straight."

"Ok. Where do we meet?"

"Right out front, I know who you are, I will get you."

So instead of taking the bus home Charlie met Derick in front of school and with four other black kids they started walking. After about five blocks two of the kids turned to another street and the remainder walked another block.

"This is my house."

Derick motioned to the second house, the other two kids crossed the street and walked on. During the walk nothing was said. There was a strange silence between all the kids.

The two turned up the walk and entered the back door. Up the stairs into the kitchen. They were greeted by a mature black woman with a questioning look on her face.

"Mama, this is Charles Knordfnerk. He is a new kid I met and since I am the first black boy he has ever met he is curious about me and black people. I know I could tell him some, but I know you could tell him a whole lot more than I ever could."

"Charlie, this is my Mama."

"It is a pleasure to meet you ma'am!"

Derick's mother looked at Charlie with amusement.

"Well young man it is a pleasure to meet you as well! What is it you are curious about? Haven't you ever seen a black boy or black people before?'

"Yes, no, well yes I have but never up close and I have never met any. Your son is the first I have met, and I want to know why white people treat black people so mean. It isn't right!"

"Well, we have a bright and inquisitive mind here Derrick. We need to fill it with the truth. First Mr. Knordfnerk, pull up a chair at our kitchen table and sit awhile and we can become acquainted."

Charlie sat down opposite Darrick's mother and paid rapt attention for over two hours. In that time, he learned about slave shipping in Africa to the southern colonies. He learned about the civil war. He learned about the emancipation proclamation. He learned about Abraham Lincoln. He learned about white supremacy and laws to deny blacks from their civil liberties. He learned about lynching of blacks by white men down south. He learned about black migration to the northern states for better jobs. He learned about white intolerance toward blacks in northern states and the ghetto's the blacks were forced to live in in most white cities. After the two plus hours and a meal he didn't even realize he had eaten she finished up by saying to Charlie.

"That is a nutshell it is what Derrick has lived with all his life and his kin for generations all the way back to when his first known Grand kin came across on a slave ship about 1700."

Charlie was dumbstruck. He never heard about slavery before and didn't know why it wasn't taught in school.

"Why don't they teach about this in school? Everyone should know about it. Everyone should know the truth!"

"Charles, dear young man, you are still innocent. You have along way to go. You have so much to learn. You can be a bright

45

star in the heavens someday. Keep up your curiosity and keep asking questions. I will be here to answer any I can, but you need to seek out better minds than mine. Keep your mind open. Meet new people. Make new and different friends. Expand your horizons. Be the best person you can be. I will keep watching you and expecting great things from you. Derrick will keep me informed about you and I expect you two will becomes friends throughout school."

"Now, young man you are long overdue to go home. I will take you there and meet your Mama and let her know what a wonderful chat we had."

With that they got up, went out to her car and she drove Charlie home.

Charlies mother and Derricks mother chatted for over an hour. When she left, she gave Charlie a gift. It was a small black notebook written in her hand containing poems she wrote in her youth about freedom. Charlie kept it as a treasure near and dear all his life.

He and Derrick did indeed become close friends all through Highschool.

HIGH SCHOOL TENTH GRADE GYM CLASS - THE SPRINT

The resident bully of the gym class, George, took on the assignment of tormenting Charlie with passion and gusto. Their lockers were across from each other's, and Charlie found himself stuck in the locker on more than one occasion. Each new day seemed to bring out a new innovation by George as he developed his techniques of torture to a science. As he was more developed than Charlie, he took great pride in degrading his adversaries poor excuse for manhood every chance he could.

"Hey dipshit, take a look at this" he stood in front of Fred and gyrated his hips to cause his penis to wave in front of Charlie's face. "You want this don't you dipshit? Take it, you'll love it. All the girls want it so you might as well too you sissy."

Somewhere in his up to now unconscious subconscious something snapped. The weeks and months of tormenting had finally caused a gasket to blow. Without thinking what he was doing Charlie took George up on his offer and grabbed his prick.

"Hey? What the hell you doing you queer"

47

With that last insulting verbal exchange Charlie got up and started walking toward the gym door with George in tow. Reaching the door, Charlie made his decision. Throwing the door open he started running and George, screaming, kept up for his life sake. One lap around the gym wasn't enough, one more time around. The girl's gym class stopped in mid exercise to cheer the marathoners on. Making a final dash back into the boy's locker room they were pursued by Mrs. Abie huffing her way after the two. They disappeared into the bowels of the boy's locker room, off limits to all women.

As they neared the showers Charlie calmly released his grip on a totally deflated George and calmly proceeded to the sinks where washed his hands. George slunk back to his locker, grabbed his cloths, and made a dash through the jeering group of boys gathered to congratulate Charlie. The slapping on his back startled and embarrassed him. He made as quick an exit as possible.

Tenth grade was going to be a challenge. Charlie didn't know anyone at Franklin except a very few kids whose families had moved to Livonia as had his during the summer.

Since he had not been able to preregister for his tenth-grade classes, he was blocked out from all the classes he wanted and needed to attend college. He was stuck with sub-par classes and was going to have to make up during summer and take extra credit classes in order to have a chance to attend the college, Michigan, that he had dreamed of going to. He took a full eight credit schedule but only six worked for him. His seventh filled a add on, choil elective and wood shop the eighth.

Charlie threw himself full bore into his classes as he was behind most students from the start and was determined to catch up by the end of the first semester. Math was no challenge nor was history. Biology opened up new horizons for him which was a delight. English brought out the poet in Charlie and he was surprised how much he liked the twists and turns it provided in ways of thinking of things. Gym was a bore but tolerable. Choir was fun and he found out he could actually sing. Woodshop was okay, but the teacher only wanted the students to make simple things to take home to mommy.

As the semester progressed Charlie found his voice and found a beautiful girl, Gwen, that drew his glance at every chance. She was the premier soprano in the choral group and as they were organizing an octet for special programs she shone through as the lead singer.

Charlie was dumbstruck when Gwen approached him on the day the finalists for the octet were to be announced and asked if he would like to join them? To his surprise she said he was the best Baritone in the choir and felt he would be a great fit. After stammering he agreed. Now he would be able to see her more and closer up. What a Bonus!

As the holiday season approached the Franklin Octet practices came every day and grew more intense. A couple students had to leave but the replacements were very good and quickly melded in.

Thanksgiving break provided an opportunity to perform at the Detroit Lions Thanksgiving Day Football Game and the rendition of the National Anthem was very well received! The great seats to watch the game were appreciated as well.

Christmas and New Year provided more opportunities to perform at senior citizen centers where Gwen and Charlie performed a new duet which went over as though they were together all their lives. It was magic and Charlie was mesmerized, particularly when Gwen gave him a kiss that smoked his eyes, ears and hair. The Chorale conductor warned them to restrain such activities afterwards, but Gwen winked at Charlie.

The second semester was a blur. Classes were more intense as Charlie put his shoulder to the grindstone to catchup as much as possible. At the end of the year, he was on a par with most of the students but still not where he wanted to be.

With Gwen he was head over heals in love but totally clumsy in his approach. They went to dances together and were inseparable, but something was missing. She was not insistent but returned his glances and didn't go out with any other boys. Everyone knew they were meant for each other, everyone except Charlie.

Summer break came and Charlie worked to make money for college so no summer fun with his friends.

ELEVENTH GRADE

Eleventh grade snuck up on Charlie and luckily all his classes came through. Even Chorale Octet! Now he was in a position to get in a position to end up in the top group at graduation and make it to University of Michigan, his dream Alma Mater. Only time would tell.

Classes took up where they had left off and Gwen/Charlie did as well. Most of their classes were the same and everywhere they went they were hand in hand. They studied together. Walked together. Talked together. They did not know anyone else existed. The year was bliss for the both of them. They finished #1 & #2 in the class at the end of the year.

Summer break came and the same routine as the previous year.

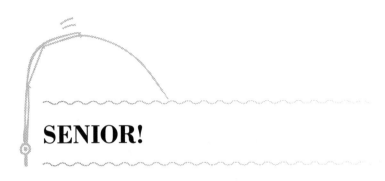

SENIOR!

Senior Year! The Year of Gwen and Charlie!
It started like a train leaving the station and picked up steam as the year went on.

No letting up!

Closer!

Faster!

Closer!

Faster!

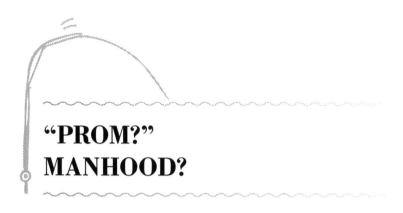

"PROM?"
MANHOOD?

" **C** ome on Chuck, what are you afraid of?"
"Everyone is doing it Chuck; you ain't a man till you do."
"Chuck, Gwen has the Hots for you. You gonna ignore her?"
"You gotta get hip Chuck."
"That thing of yours is going to rot off if you don't use it." On and on it went from his "buds". You would think the only thing that went on in high school was sex. What with all the flower children and hippies espousing free love it did seem all pervasive.

Charlie was at that awkward age, the tweens. He was a teen in body but much too immature in mind. He still preferred the old fishing hole with Paul to having anything to do with girls. What was all the fuss about anyway? He was sure that someday he might be interested in girls just not yet.

Charlie had not had the "Talk" from either of his parents. Gertrude was adamant that Neezer do it and Neezer was not about to talk about anything as personal as having sex. May haps Charlie was better off not gaining his parents instructions in this matter.

As his senior year wended it way towards graduation the pressure mounted. Jeff and John, the two most respected and feared seniors, took it on themselves to have Chuck's cherry busted before graduation. Never had there been a stranger trio. The two jocks of the class destined for greatness or prison depending on your viewpoint and the most pathetic gawky testament to abstinence in the class of 1965. For some strange reason they worked well together, and no one ever questioned if Charlie fit in. At least not to Jeff or John.

No one knew which of the two, Jeff or John came up with the scheme, but it appeared to be destined to change the annals of prom night at Franklin High School for all eternity. It was simplicity in itself. Jeff and John bought the tickets and threatened Charlie with life and limb if he didn't go. Gwen being enamored with the chance was more than willing to take on the challenge. Everything was set. Jeff and John picked Charlie up in the "Babe Box", a beat up half dead delivery van, at the appointed time. The girls were waiting at Gwen's home and piled in without the "B-B" even having to stop. Off to the Raleigh House for a night to remember. All went as planned. Charlie danced (if you could call it that) with Gwen all night and was growing more and more enthusiastic with the thought of culminating his high school career with the conquest of Gwen. Particularly with the help of the punch Jeff and John kept feeding him.

As midnight approached Jeff and John guided the two staggering lovebirds out to the "B-B" and stood guard. Gwen was all over Charlie, and he returned the favor clumsily. As the moment of passion neared Charlie remembered the gift from his ol fishing bud Paul. Rising and reaching for his trousers he fumbled in the pocket and came up with his quest. Gwen was beside herself with passion and curiosity as Charlie exposed the item of the minute. "It's a Polish Condom", he explained. A look of horror crossed Gwen's face as she realized what Charlie was about to do.

It is said people two miles away wondered what the primordial scream was that night. Had some animal met its maker?

Polish condoms are excellent at birth control but better suited for their designed purpose, clamping papers together not penises.

GREETINGS

The summer of Charlie's graduation came and went. Hot and devoid of anything of interest until "The Letter "arrived. "Greetings form your president. You are hereby ordered to report to Fort Wayne, Detroit Michigan on August 9 for induction into the United States Armed Forces."

No college this year?

No college this year!

No escape. No fleeing to Canada as a few of the kids he knew had done. He faced his duty as his brother and father had done before. With pride and fear he reported to the front desk of the induction station and was directed down the hall.

Charlie joined a long line of young men and waited his turn. Tall, short, skinny, fat, blacks, whites, the cream of Americas youth looking like lambs being led to the slaughter. All with the look of a deer caught in headlights.

Directed into a large room each man was directed to a table and chair where there was a group of papers neatly stacked in front of each chair. Told to sit and await further instructions some of the men started going through the paperwork.

"You are about to get a court martial if you touch any of those papers again before being instructed to do so." Screamed a soldier in a uniform with more stripes than Charlie ever thought he would ever see again. Ram rod straight and dressed in a uniform that looked like it was about to break when he moved Staff Sergeant Kelly strode through the hall, a cloud of fear surrounding him.

"You rejects from a shit farm are mine now. Your mamas aren't going to help you wipe your asses now so get this straight, I am your mother and father and your God all rolled up into one and I don't take any shit from scum."

Having the devout attention of every cruit there the sergeant strode to the front of the room, planted his feet and stared down his nose at the cruits nearest him. "When I tell you to do so you will pick up the pencils in front of you and fill out the first and only the first paper in front of you. When you are done with the first paper you will hold your hand with pencil high in the air till you are instructed to proceed with the next paper. Any questions? I thought not." The few hands that had started to rise quickly dropped.

"Ready, begin the first and only the first paper." With that the cruits started filling out the paper. Those who were eager to impress quickly completed theirs while others struggled with their answers. The first lesson of military life quickly sunk in as several young men had to hold their pencils high for over twenty minutes. The first to waiver having been hit by the sergeant's swagger stick ensured all would comply.

When the last man raised his hand, the sergeant instructed the cruits to start on the second paper. There were no eager beavers raising their hands quickly from there on in.

Two hours later all the paperwork had been completed in an orderly fashion and the cruits were directed out of the room into a locker room where they were instructed to remove their clothing and keeping only their skivvies and shoes on and proceed to the physical room. Each cruit was prodded, poked, inoculated, squeezed and directed to turn their heads and cough. Thoroughly humiliated they were led back into the locker room and instructed to dress and return to the room where the paperwork nightmare had started. Only two cruits were excused. This was war time; you had to be near death not to be accepted in Uncle Sam's service.

The cruits were separated into three groups. Marines to the left, Army center and Navy to the right. The Air Force didn't need any draftees.

A high-ranking officer entered the room and Staff Sergeant Kelly yelled "Attention." Every man stood to attention to the best of his knowledge. The officer approached a microphone and addressed the gathered recruits. "Gentlemen, I am General Thacary McClelland, and it is my honor and pleasure to swear you into the armed forces of the United States of America. You will repeat after me."

Within two minutes Charlie and the hoard of cannon fodder were soldiers, sailors, or marines. No trumpets. No drums. No applause form admiring throngs to see them off.

The men were marshaled into three groups and marched to the Pick Fort Shelby Hotel where they were fed a sumptuous meal the likes they would not see till they were discharged at the end of their tours of duty.

From the hotel they were marched to the old train station where they were loaded onto three different trains, one headed west to Great Lakes Naval boot camp. One train headed east to Quantico Marine boot camp and Charlie's train headed south to Fort Knox for Army basic training.

Arriving early the next morning Charlie tasted his first dose of "Hell".

"Alright you shit for brains scum, get off this train now and get into formation out there." The men scrambled off the train and got into what they thought was a pretty good formation. At least they were all in one place. "You morons line up in four ranks and make them straight. I know you are too stupid to understand much so you will all turn to your right now." Some poor fool turned left and was harangued by the sergeant nose to nose with the recruit's face being soaked not by sweat but the sergeant's verbiage.

Being all basically facing in the same direction the recruits were marched off to the reception station. Each man was required to strip and place all his belongings into a green cloth bag and carry it with him. Again, the recruits were prodded, poked, squeezed and manipulated by Army Doctors and medics. They entered a room where they were all lined up into four ranks and Charlie found himself in the front rank near the middle.

"Attention you scum, Major Doctor Zilke is going to examine you for hernias. You will all now drop your drawers. When the Major is in front of you turn your head to the side and cough when instructed to do so and not before. Do not cough into the Doctors face or you will not be pleased by the outcome."

As the Major, proceeded along the line Charlie was startled to realize the Major was a woman and a very large one at that. He guessed she could hold her own against most men in the group.

Two soldiers directly behind Charlie were enjoying the proceedings as the first group of recruits was extremely embarrassed when they realized the Major was a woman and their egos were dealt a formidable blow.

The soldier directly behind Charlie whispered to his buddy, "Watch this."

The Major arrived in front of him and glancing down turned purple and exclaimed "You pig." With that she raised her clipboard and striking downward encountered an object that gave off a sickening splat sound. Charlie looked puzzled. The young man behind him turned ashen gray then purple and collapsed.

After a long grueling day, the new soldiers to be were released to their barracks where most took showers prior to hitting their racks. Laughing and joking with each other as the showers were winding down Charlie found a sense of camaraderie he had never known.

These guys had gone through the same ordeal as him and they had survived the day together. This was not going to be so bad after all. His soap slipped out of his hands and hit the floor. As he picked it up a sudden look of total surprise crossed his face. A familiar face from the rank behind him was there again but this time with a look of retribution and revenge on that face.

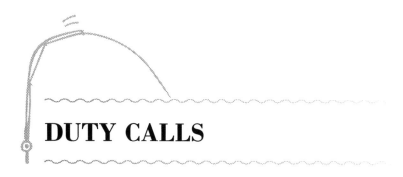

DUTY CALLS

The life of a soldier was not what he had expected. Having scored well on his entry tests he found himself in Medic School after basic training. This was much better than the bulk of his Cruit buddies who were sent on to infantry training with the prospects of becoming cannon fodder in "Nam."

Upon graduation from AIT Charlie was allowed to pick his duty assignment as a reward for being the top graduate in his class.

Germany sounded much better than Viet Nam so off to Augsburg, Deutschland he went. Augsburg, home of the 24th Infantry Division was as good as Charlie thought he could ever get. Working with Doctors in the brigade aid station was a cushy job and the few field treks when the units went out on maneuvers were hardly a hardship.

Rotating every three months for one month in the hospital was a treat appreciated by all the medics. The hospital had more than its share of women and even though Charlie still had not reached "full manhood" he did appreciate English speaking women.

Duty in Germany was euphoric with one exception. The commanding General of the 24th Division was an egomaniac with a penchant of making life miserable for anyone within a two-mile radius.

Major General Thaddeus Engler had been under suspicion of theft of historical artifacts wherever he had been assigned and Germany was no different. The Army was about to unceremoniously dump the General if he didn't voluntarily retire at a one-star rank. Rather than face a possible court marshal and be forced out and the humiliation that would entail he accepted his fate. This, however, did not stop the good General from shipping about one ton of Nazi artifacts back to the states.

The battalion Charlie was assigned to for field duty, the 2nd Battalion of the 70th Armor Brigade received the dubious honor of packing and shipping the General's "Household Goods". Charlie accompanied his unit on their "field duty" to provide medical aid if needed. He thought it strange that two sets of "goods" were crated and shipped. One set went to Manhattan Kansas, the Generals home, containing cow manure and one set was shipped to the Embassy in Afghanistan. Someone was not going to be very happy opening one of the sets of crates.

As the end of his tour of duty approached General Engler was required to check into the Army Hospital for a full examination. As the examination was to take three days the good General was given the royal treatment with a plush private room reserved for dignitaries. His meals were sumptuous, and his treatment was superb.

Charlie made an out of schedule trip to the hospital to cover for a buddy going on a three-day pass. Gaining access to the Generals room was no problem for someone able to coax the best fish out of the Huron River.

Knocking on the general's door Charlie entered attired in his hospital whites. Clipboard in hand he apologized for the intrusion and explained he was there to take the Generals vitals. Grumbling the General gave his arm for the blood pressure check and pulse taking then opened his mouth for the thermometer. Charlie balked and stammered that the doctors wanted a rectal temperature as they were concerned about an anomaly and wanted a comparative temperature for safety. "I'm sorry General, I'll just take your temperature the regular way and enter the results as the other way."

"Soldier, the Army works like a well-oiled machine because of orders followed so you will do as the doctors ordered and proceed."

The General turned sunny side up and Charlie inserted the device. "Sir, I'll just step out of the room for a moment and be right back to complete my rounds so you can have your privacy."

Grumbling the General nodded, and Charlie exited the room.

The door opened about two minutes later and a voice yelled, "Hey General." Turning his head, the General was blinded by a bright flash and was never able to identify the intruder.

A strange photograph was posted all over the base the next day. A figure lying on a hospital bed with two stars on the foot of the bed was turned to face the camera. A cigar was clenched in his teeth and a daisy was protruding from his rectum. The caption under the picture said it all, "Goodbye General Engler".

No perpetrators were ever charged.

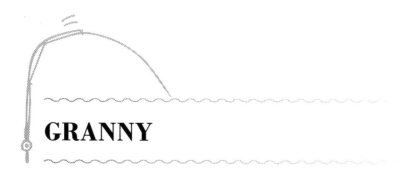

GRANNY

Six months prior to being discharged from the Army Charlie found himself transferred to Fort Leonard Wood, Mo. Duty was easy in the post hospital and the six months flew by.

After two years of service to his country he was a free man. A buddy gave him a lift to the bus station in Waynesville, Mo. for the trip home. As he rode to the bus station, he noticed an ornate Victorian house on the edge of town a sign at the roadside proclaimed "Granny's House. Your wildest dreams fulfilled". After purchasing a ticket to St. Louis for a flight home Charlie decided to utilize his two hours wait testing Granny's wildest dreams. Leaving his duffle bag at the bus station he caught a cab to Granny's.

Entering the front door to the most beautiful house he had ever seen he was greeted by Granny. An ancient 4-foot gray haired apparition dressed to the nines greeted Charlie and inquired as to his wildest dreams. "Well, I have never had sex in my life, so I was hoping to get screwed before I went home."

"Your wish is my command. Just go down the hallway to the

second door on the left and you will get your wish. That will be twenty dollars."

Charlie fished a crisp new $20.00 from his wallet handed it to Granny and proceeded down the hall to the second door on the left. Gathering his breath, he entered the door which promptly closed behind him. A puzzled Charlie found himself outside in a garden and turning noticed a sign on the door proclaiming, "You have just been screwed by Granny!"

He returned to the station to await his bus to St Louis.

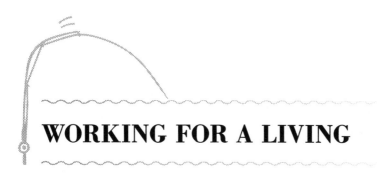

WORKING FOR A LIVING

Life after the Army was something new. Having gone to the Army right out of High School and not having a usable skill as he saw it, he didn't know what kind of work he wanted to do. All his friends from high school were either still in the Army, away at school or kicking around working at the local A & P. Charlie thought about school but determined he wanted to find his vocation before he committed to four years of school.

He bounced around several jobs from working in a nursing home where he found his military skills useless to working as a laborer on construction sites. The latter was more to his liking, and he thought he might like to get into an apprenticeship or go to school to become an engineer. The camaraderie of the construction sites reminded him of his Army life, and he felt comfortable in that atmosphere. It was good honest work and it paid well.

One problem remained though; Charlie was still a virgin, a horny one at that. He was at wits end and about to blow a gasket. Every time he entered a porta-john on a construction site the porta-john was seen to shake. He found it necessary to relieve himself every time he was alone. Carrying a well-worn copy of Playboy everywhere he went was the norm.

While working on the Wyandotte City Powerhouse during an addition and renovation he found himself getting extremely agitated. The frequency of relief trips was getting noticed by everyone. As Charlie approached the locker room/restroom a group of workers were looking over a set of blueprints one of the workers was holding against the wall. When he entered the door, the workers left suddenly. Entering a stall, he produced his copy of the December 1968 issue of Playboy and went to work. Within minutes the desired outcome arrived to a cheering throng. Looking up Charlie discovered to his horror that the roof of the restroom was missing. About 50 construction workers were arrayed along three floors of powerhouse mezzanine cheering and applauding his accomplishment. Grabbing his trousers and making a beeline for the exit he passed a notice next to the door which read, "Restroom closed for renovation, use locker room only." Too bad the notice had been covered by a blueprint when he entered.

Strange reasons often precede pay checks being mailed out.

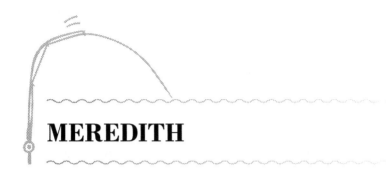

MEREDITH

Meredith was an enigma. Charlie had met dozens of women in his life and been tongue tied with them all until Meredith. There was an intangible something that attracted him since he first met her at the Nightcap Bar on 6 Mile at Salem. There was a feeling like he had known her all his life. She felt like an old buddy. For the first time he was comfortable with a woman, and it felt good.

They started dating in August and their attraction and affection grew steadily.

Meredith's parents were going to be away for the holiday's, and she invited Charlie to join her at their summer cabin in Traverse City. Just the two of them in a comfy north woods log cabin on Lake Michigan.

Charlie grew increasingly eager as the Christmas week approached; His imagination ran wild. All his hopes and dreams would be fulfilled at long last.

Friday evening arrived and like clockwork Meredith showed up in her Mercedes Bens 500 SEL. The trip would be in comfort and style.

The trip was uneventful but not boring in the least. They talked about anything and everything and found their passions and dislikes were incredibly similar. The four hours flew by.

As they pulled up to the house Charlie was stunned. Wrapped in a pristine blanket of new snow was the most beautiful and largest log home he had ever seen. Meredith had called it their summer cabin, but it had to exceed 10,000 square feet. The house was perched on a bluff overlooking a frozen Grand Traverse Bay. The property was about 400 acres of the finest grapes to be found on the Old Mission peninsula.

On entering the home Charlie was overwhelmed by the magnitude, the magnificence and the comfortable warmth the home exuded.

Touches of Meredith's family were everywhere. Homey touches, not austentatious. Pictures of family were located throughout the home but not overbearing. Fishing trips, cruises, exotic places were represented. Meredith's parent's favorite place, New Zealand, where they were spending the holidays was well represented.

Being exhausted they both agreed to get a good night's rest and see what would be on the morrow. Blissful sleep came quickly.

A sparkling morning greeted Charlie. After a brisk refreshing shower, he found his way to the dining room where a sumptuous breakfast was laid out.

"Hey sleepy head, I thought I was going to have to come up and drag you out of bed."

The day's itinerary was planned over crepes, fresh fruit, Irish Oatmeal and the best coffee Charlie had ever tasted.

Touring the open tourist haunts in town, lunch at a great pub, a few hours donating to the local Indian Casino then to the Grand Traverse Inn for a five-star meal.

Seven P.M. found the couple back at the "Cabin" basking in front of cozy fire on a bear skin rug. As temperatures rose and the fire died down, they found their way to Meredith's bedroom. As Meredith went into her bathroom to prepare herself, he explored the suite. The usual accoutrements were there to be found. Favorite toys, books, family pictures, etc. A new picture caught Charlie's eye, a young man in his early twenties. Charlie felt uncomfortable seeing the picture but didn't know why.

Meredith emerged from her dressing room adorned in a beautiful negligee and gown. She turned the lights down low then came to him. Slowly she unbuttoned his shirt and removing it lay it across the arm of a chair. Next his trousers were lowered. Meredith playfully started kissing Charlie on the arms, neck then cheek as he was slowly reduced to his shorts.

Meredith let drop her gown and slowly pulled him to her bed. Noticing a picture of the same young man on the headboard Charlie couldn't help but ask, "Meredith, are you married?"

"No, never been married" she retorted. Still curious he asked, "Is that your boyfriend?"

"No, that's not my boyfriend."

Still uncomfortable about the picture Charlie pursued the topic between ever more passionate ministrations from Meredith.

"Is that your brother?"

A breathless and highly aroused Meredith replied, "NO!"

Overcome by an unreasonable nagging curiosity Charlie blurted out, "Who the hell is that guy?"

Meredith, rising up on one elbow, a twinkle in her eye, looking at Charlie in an impish way replied. "Why silly, that's me before my surgery."

It was an agonizing bus ride back to Detroit.

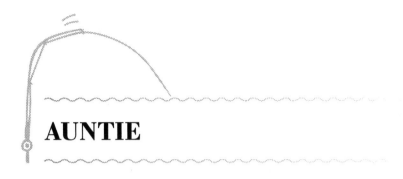

AUNTIE

Charlie had not seen his Great Aunt Elva in over 15 years. He had been 8 or nine when she had moved to New York. Elva had been something of a black sheep of the family, married five times and something of a wild woman in her day. Now in her eighties she had mellowed, or so the family believed.

Elva had made a name for herself having been the first woman to hold a drivers license in the state of Michigan. She was also the first woman to wreck a car and lose her license. She had run rum across the border with Canada with her second husband, or was that her third? Marijuana had found its way into her pipe on numerous occasions long before the love generation. Other oddities were never related to Charlie.

Charlie had wanted to see the Empire State building and the statue of Liberty. Since he was going to be in New York he thought he might as well look up his Great Aunt. Elva lived in a non-descript brownstone on the east side of central park. It was a nice enough neighborhood with few shootings or muggings.

Elva greeted Charlie with open arms. "My dear boy, you have

grown into quite a man. You were only about this high the last time I saw you." As usual he found himself drawn close to his Great Aunt as she had been the only person who allowed him to get away with mischievous pranks whenever he had been at her home in Michigan. Her fifth husband, George, always scolded Charlie but Elva protected him and let him get away with everything.

Elva invited him to go out on the town with her but first she had to make a trip to the bank. She brought forth an old satchel from her closet and off they went to the bank. Charlie waited patiently with Elva in line exchanging gossip about the family and happenings therein bringing Elva up to date. When they got to the teller the young man asked how he might help her today. "I would like to open an account at your bank with three million dollars." The teller laughed as he was handed the satchel. His face became ghostly white, and his jaw dropped when he looked inside. "Madam, I'm going to have to have my manager help you with this. Please wait here one moment." He moved hurriedly to his manager's desk. The two talked shortly, the manager investigated the satchel then at Elva. He picked up a phone and talked with someone for a few seconds. The teller and the manager both came to the teller's window. "Madam, I would be pleased to have you meet our president as he would like to personally assist you in opening your account, if that is all right with you?"

"Of course, young man, where is he?"

"This way madam, I'll escort you up to his office."

Charlie and Aunt Elva were escorted around the teller's row to an elevator where they were whisked up to the penthouse offices of the president of the bank.

They were greeted by a pleasant secretary who informed

them the president was waiting for them. Entering the president's office Charlie was awed by its opulence and size. Wealth oozed everywhere. An older, portly, nattily attired man approached them and greeted them warmly. "Welcome to Chaise Manhattan Bank Madam, I am please to meet you." The president directed them to the most comfortable couch Charlie had ever sat on. With a short nod from the president the manager who had escorted them gave a short bow and left the office.

"I understand you would like to open an account with us for quite a large sum of money, is that right?"

"Yes, it is and here is my deposit." With that Elva handed the president her satchel which he opened. Peering inside his eyes bugged out and he glanced up with a puzzled look. "My dear lady, how did you come to have such a large sum of money?"

"I've saved over the years and made several very good bets."

"You mean investments?"

"No, bets. I bet on sure things and always win."

"What kind of bets do you make?"

"Oh, just about anything, for example I bet you that by ten tomorrow morning your testicles will be square. I'll bet you $50,000.00 and I never lose."

A startled look morphed and a greedy grin crossed the president's face as he replied. "Madam, I will take you up on your wager. My testicles are not square now nor will they be by ten tomorrow morning."

"All right young man, I and my nephew will be here at nine thirty sharp tomorrow morning to collect my bet." With that Aunt Elva got up from the couch and started toward the door.

"Aren't you forgetting something madam? Don't you want to open an account with us?"

"I'll take care of that tomorrow morning, good day to you." With that she exited the office, took the elevator down and left the building with Charlie in tow.

"Aunt Elva, do you really have three million dollars?"

"That's all I brought with me today honey, I didn't think I needed any more."

Charlie was stunned into silence. There was little talking between the two as they visited the sights of New York before they found their way back to Aunt Elva's home. Charlie was nervous the entire time knowing there was an old satchel containing three million dollars loosely draped over Aunt Elva's arm two feet from him in one of the toughest cities in the world. Elva on the other hand was totally relaxed.

That evening Aunt Elva made several phone calls till she got the answer she wanted. With a satisfied smile on her face, she bid him good night. "We will have a busy day tomorrow Charles so get a good night's sleep."

With that she left him to wonder about the day's happenings and look forward to the morrow's adventures. He drifted off to sleep.

Bright and early Aunt Elva woke Charlie. Breakfast was ready and waiting. "You want to sleep the day away Charles? There is money to be made today. Can't wait for the poorhouse."

He wolfed down his breakfast and was ready when Aunt Elva was. "There will one other person going with us today. He should be here any moment now."

As if choreographed the doorbell rang startling Charlie. Aunt Elva answered the door and a man in his mid thirties entered.

"My chariot awaits you madam, shell we go?"

"Charles, this is Mr. Schlab, just like his grandfather."

Charlie shook hands with the man, and they headed out to Mr. Schlab's waiting limo.

At nine thirty they entered the main branch of Chase Manhattan Bank and were escorted up to the president's office where they were greeted by a haggard looking president. It seems the president had spent a fitful knight tossing and turning worrying about his testicles. He had taken great care protecting them from anything that could possibly cause them to become square.

The president smiled at Charlie and gave a puzzled glance at the man Aunt Elva had brought along.

"This is my broker; I hope you don't mind but I include him in all my large transactions."

"There is no problem at all Madam, but I must inform you that you are going to lose your bet today."

"Oh well, I must see for myself if you don't mind."

"Oh but of course."

With that the president turned his back to the group and dropped his trousers. Aunt Elva moved around him, bent over and peered at his crotch. She looked up at the clock and just before ten o'clock reached over and grabbed the president by the balls.

"There, I told you madam, my testicles are perfectly normal."

"They are indeed young man, I guess I lost that bet. That's the first bet I have lost in a very long time."

While they were completing their tête-à-tête, the president noticed Mr. Schlab banging his head against the wall. "What, pray tell, is wrong with your broker?"

"Oh him, well it seems I made a bet with him that I would have the president of Chase Manhattan Bank by the balls by ten o'clock this morning and I won that bet."

"And if I may ask how much that was bet madam?"

"Oh, that was a measly one hundred thousand dollars. You see I never really lose a bet."

The president of Chase Manhattan bank was rolling on the floor, but poor Mr. Schlab was blubbering like a baby. A sprightly Aunt Elva simply smiled, gathered her satchel and led her broker out of the office after placing a bundle of large bills on the president's desk.

GWEN AGAIN

Drowning oneself in remorse via the nearest tavern often proceeds from self-humiliation and Charlie was no exception. Seven and Seven became the drink de jour. Eight or ten usually did the trick. Comforting fog became a frequent occurrence till a typical twist repeated in his life. Two old acquaintances appeared out of no where to the relief of a lonely young man.

Charlie found himself next to Jeff and John one evening. Milking their drinks and on the prowl for pink taco the two were surprised and pleased to renew their friendship. Neither had been in the military and hadn't done much with their lives other than work at the Ford Wixom plant and spent their nights chasing tail.

The night sped by as the trio regaled each other with remembrances. John and Jeff had kept track or their scores and boasted or their numerous conquests, three hundred eighty-five for John to three hundred seventy-nine for Jeff. It seems Jeff had caught something that slowed him down for a month or so allowing John to surpass him. Thankfully the two were too busy with their boasts to inquire as to Chuck's count. It did come out that Chuck was currently not seeing anyone though.

It was Jeff who came up with the idea of a group date and he knew the perfect date for Chuck. Gwen was recently divorced, and wouldn't it be grand for the old group to get together, like the old days, at Kensington Park for a picnic and whatever came up? Reluctantly Charlie agreed. The Friday after Memorial Day would be perfect, but he first would have to become reacquainted with Gwen.

Wednesday nights were stand-up comedy nights at the Continental Lounge in Wixom and Gwen usually attended. John and Jeff talked Chuck into showing up for the next comedy session. He was looking forward to rekindling what ever flame there had once been and atoning for the phuba of long ago.

The week seemed to last forever. Charlie's anticipation of seeing Gwen was palpable.

If records were kept for clock watching it would be his. Every clock encountered was checked and double checked. The face on his watch was worn out from his tapping on it to make sure it was still running.

Everyone encountered was asked for the time.

Monday dragged on...

Tuesday time died.

Wednesday the clocks fluctuated from going forward to running backward.

Thursday crept by at a snail's pace.

Friday was the first 72hour day in the history of mankind. Eternity came and went before 4:30 arrived.

A mad dash in slow motion traffic got Charlie home.

Shower!

Shave! (Please Lord, no nicks or cuts tonight, please!)

Aftershave.

Deodorant.

Cleaning teeth tongue and gums.

Trim the nose hairs.

Brylcream, "A little dab will do ya".

Tee shirt.

Drawers, boxers or briefs? Briefs!

Socks, wow, they even matched.

Six shirts later, perfect.

New slacks.

Shoes? Dang, they need polishing. Dang, got polish on my shirt. Two shirts later, ok, ready to go.

Checked breath again, still ok.

Checked the hair, still ok.

Checked clock, 5:30.

Checked house, still neat and clean. "Boy I hope I get lucky tonight!"

The Doorbell!

Josh & Jeff were here!

A surreal ride in the backseat to the bar.

Josh & Jeff's dates were there and already ensconced in their first drinks.

A second round of drinks.

Charlie, drifting in and out of the conversation, eyes focused on the front door.

The 37th time the front door opened she appeared. Gwen! She was just as beautiful as he remembered.

"Hi guys, Hi Charlie" A peck on the cheek?

"I want you guys to meet my friend Carol. We met last week."

The most passionate kiss Charlie had ever seen. Smoke, sparks, music, WOW!

Stunned silence. Josh, Jeff and their dates turned red.

Charlie was mesmerized.

The longest night of his life ended at 7:00 P.M.

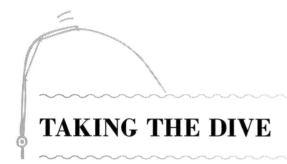

TAKING THE DIVE

A nother summer went by. Another winter went by.
"Charles, go somewhere, do something"

"Come on Chuck, get a hobby, put some life in your life."

"Chuck, do you want to go to the ballgame tonight?"

"Hey Chuck, let's go bowling."

Charlies mother was becoming worried her son was becoming too reclusive and suggested he take up a hobby to get him involved with other people. Taking her advice, he pursued several activities but found none to his liking. After several fruitless forays into fishing, bridge clubs, square dancing, fencing, etc. he gave up.

"Charlie, did you see that SCUBA program on TV last night? The second half is on tonight. Check it out. That looks really cool."

Charlie had watched Lloyd Bridges for year. This was new. This was different. Jacque Cousteau was the inventor of SCUBA, and his films struck a chord with Charlie. Serenity, peace and privacy all rolled up into one great hobby.

Charlie was glued to the set. This was him. This is what he needed. Searching the Detroit area was fruitless, there were no dive schools around. He had noticed an article in Playboy about scuba diving and the babes in the sport. Doing a little investigating he found a school run by one of the article's babes in Oregon. "Come dive in Oregon." The pamphlet read. Pictures of lakes surrounded by mountains enticed him. The phone number beckoned him. Finally, he called in late March.

"Kathy's Dive School & Shop the voice on the other end said. "Kathy here, how may I help you?"

"Hi, my name is Charlie and I saw your ad in "Diving World", and I want to learn to dive.

"I'm sorry sir but all our classes are booked up this year. I could put you on a waiting list in case there is a cancellation, or I could sign you up for next year."

"Ah, OK, put me on your list. My name is Charles Knordfnerk, and my address and phone number are *******"

Kathy wrote down all the information and for some unknown reason put his name on the top of the list of names waiting for an opening to the dive school.

Charlie hadn't hung up ten minutes and was half-heartedly looking at the other dive school ads when the phone startled him.

"Charles, you won't believe this, but I just got a cancellation for the class starting July 24, can you make that one?"

"Yes, that would be great. Do you need a deposit or what?"

"No, the canceller said to donate the nonrefundable deposit and I thought of you. I will send all the information you will need to your address. There will be a list of motels and inn's, but I suggest Fred & Ethyl's cabins about a mile from here."

"Great, thank you, thank you!"

"You are welcome. I will see you in July. Goodbye for now."

"Thanks again and goodbye for now."

He applied and was scheduled to attend the class starting on July 24.

This was new. This was for him. He bought every book he could find on the subject and read them over and over. Jacque Cousteau became his hero. He joined the WMCA and started swimming every day. He often had to be chased out of the pool at closing time. Not since his Army days had he been so fit. This was going to be it. Serenity, peace and privacy all rolled up into one great hobby.

April became May became June became July.

On July 21 he caught a flight to Portland. Descending into Portland was always interesting. Seeing Mt. Hoods majesty above the low clouds was inspiring. The crazy 450* left hand spiral down to the airport quickened his pulse and heightened his senses of being alive. Rental car in gear, maps in hand, bags in the trunk. With a warning from the rental people of possible detours due to forest fires he headed south.

Sure, enough a detour required him to divert to highway 101 and south down the coast. Charlie was enchanted by the beauty of the area. The roiling Pacific on his right, beautiful mountains to his left. In Coos Bay he found the best clam chowder he had ever eaten at a place called Mo's. Four hours later he pulled into Oroville. He took up residence in Fred & Ethyl's Cabins and made himself acquainted with the area. Three days of sightseeing gave Charlie a new appreciation for beauty. It was beautiful mountainous country and the dive school utilized Lake Oroville for the finale certification dives.

At the appointed time he showed up at the dive shop for his training. To his disappointment the class was taught by a snaggletooth woman on the north side of 50. The first two days were taken up with classroom work and becoming familiar with practices and equipment. Day three with the first introduction with the pool and use of the equipment came and along with it was the main instructor, Kathy. It was love at first sight for Charlie. She was the most beautiful sight he had ever seen, 5' – 6", auburn hair, voluptuous, a goddess.

Charlie had a difficult time concentrating on her instruction. Several times Kathy had to backtrack to make sure he was up with the class. The practice dives in the pool went fairly well and he became adept with the buddy system and sharing one tank for emergency use and other procedures. He did more swimming in that week than he had since his days fishing on the Huron River. The second week was even more swimming and running thrown into the mix. On Wednesday there was an event called the "Swim-off". The principal swimming coach was Frank, late of the Navy Seals. Every student was to complete 100 laps. Two of the class had already dropped out so the six remaining would swim against Frank. After lunch everyone was in the pool and the swim-off began. There was no contest. Frank swam effortlessly leaving the class in his wake. At 2:30 Frank pulled himself out of the pool only to find Charlie sitting on the edge having finished his 100 laps five minutes earlier. The other five students were called out of the pool; and told they could finish their laps in the morning.

Frank invited Charlie to go for a run with him. After five miles they arrived back at the dive shop

Shaking his hand Frank bid Charlie "Good evening, see you in the morning".

As he pulled out of the parking lot Kathy came out and stood next to Frank watching Charlie's car disappear around the bend.

"Well, what do you think Frank?'

"I think you have found my replacement."

"Maybe, we'll see. We still have the deep-water test tomorrow."

Thursday morning and a ten-mile run for the three remaining students along with Frank. The other students were forgiven their remaining laps since they had proven themselves for endurance. Now came the hardest part of the training, deep water.

Frank was a very tough taskmaster as he explained, "There are very few 2nd chances if you screw up when you are 100 feet below the surface."

The students were drilled and re-drilled in emergency procedures in deep water. What to do if your equipment failed. What to do if your buddy panics. What to do if someone gets injured. What to do if you get injured.

Films of nitrogen narcosis, the "Bends" were shown. First aid was gone over again and again.

After a light lunch everyone was in the deep-water tank. Each student paired with Frank then with each other with Frank giving encouragement and corrections.

At 4:00 Frank called it a day and congratulated everyone for great work and gave them a map to the location for their final test dive on Friday.

On Thursday of the second week the longstanding tradition was to meet at the Brew Barn at 7:00 P.M. for the standup comedy contest. All the class, including Kathy, met at the Brew Barn to have a few drinks and talk about the weeks training and make fools of themselves.

The pub was known for its standup comedy attempts. One by one patrons got up and attempted to make it to three minutes. The norm was for them to get booed off the stage well before.

The emcee challenged the dive class and its instructors to give it a try. They would only have to make it to two minutes. The first two made it to one minute when they got the hook. They at least got polite catcalls. Kathy was called up, rather pushed up and red-faced began.

"Back in the day we didn't have sex education in school like they do now. We had to learn it the hard way. We had to go behind the barn and watch the animals do it then we had to practice what we saw. Let me tell you, chickens have it hard, but I think goats are queer.

That brings me to the hope of all mankind. We are told we evolved but after working with my current dive class I do not believe there is any hope for this primordial soup I have had to work with."

As she exited with applause, not from the students but the patrons, she pointed at Charlie. "You, up there, NOW!"

Charlie was pushed up onto the stage where he promptly made a pratfall to the amusement of everyone.

Dusting himself off, he cleared his throat and began.

"Many of you here are accustomed to cold weather but how many of you are accustomed to swimming in cold weather? There is an old custom in Michigan of swimming in Lake Superior in January. If you have the courage and can get it done, you become a member of the "Gitchigumi Swimmers". It has to be witnessed and sworn to by an honest person or repute and only about 1% of attempters succeed. Last year my girlfriend and I found ourselves at Copper Harbor on January 17. The temperature was a balmy -6 or there abouts. We stripped and on the count of two, couldn't wait for three, we jumped in an open hole in the ice. I don't know if we entered the water or bounced but we were out rather quickly.

Extreme cold does strange things to the human body. For one it was hard to tell who was male or female. My nipples were bigger than hers and her clit was bigger than my penis. Besides she had more hair on her chest than I did."

Cheers greeted Charlie as he was about to leave the stage when the emcee called him for one more

"I would like to introduce you to my father but alas he is no longer with us. We often frequented places like this. He loved his Stroh's Beer. I remember fondly his 80th birthday as I took him to our local bordello. He is being shy and unsure what to do after all the idle years had to be assisted. The madam helped him select a pretty young thing, Blond and built for action. She was leading him to her room and asked him if he were kinky. "No." he replied "But I do have to ask a favor of you"

"Sure, what is it?"

"Well, would you please stand on your head when we do it?"

"I knew you were kinky", she laughed.

"No dear, you don't understand. When you get my age, you don't stick it in anymore, you drop it in."

They entered her room to the cheers of the other Ladies of the Night.

As he started to get off the stage the emcee came out and pushed him back up to the cheers and applause of the audience.

"Chuck, you have to give us more than that, you broke the dive clubs record.

He smiled and looking at Kathy started talking. "I will always cherish the last bit of advice my father gave to me. He said, "Son there are three things I want you to remember to your dying day. First, never pass a bathroom, second, never waste a hard-on and third, never, ever trust a fart."

More cheers erupted than had ever been heard to the delight of the emcee. He pulled Charlie aside and asked if he had anything up his sleeve. Charly whispered into his ear and with a puzzled look he nodded.

The audience howled as he left the stage.

After five minutes the emcee called a halt to the bad fruit of ill spent labor and announced a special request was about to be performed for their finale.

Charlie came up on stage with Kathy and whispered to her what they were going to do. She laughed and nodded.

A bed was rolled our and Kathy and Charlie climbed under the sheet.

The emcee announced, "We are about to find out how the first sign language procreation was performed. Ladies and Gentlemen, Charlie and Kathy!"

The sheet started moving, Charlie turned towards a sleeping Kathy and shook her shoulder. Shrugging him off he shook her again. She turned and giving him a look of disgust, shrugged her shoulders and started to turn back. Charlie tapped her and pulled out a street sign, "One Way" in an arrow. Kathy pulled out a "Do Not Enter" sign and started to turn back. Charlie tapped her again and held up a "Yield" sign which immediately caused her to pull out a "Stop" sign out and turn back over. Charlie sat looking puzzled for a few seconds then gave a look of "Eureka", pulled a hand made Michigan I-69 sign and shook her again. Kathy sat up with a mad look till she saw the sign, raised her arms and embraced Charlie whereupon they dove back under the sheet to the cheers of the audience. The emcee approached the bed laughing and started to pull the sheet back. A surprised look joined the laughter he emitted, and the bed was pulled off the stage. Charlie and Kathy came out from behind the curtains returning to their table. the audience cheered and whistled with admiration. The emcee came over and he cancelled their bill he enjoyed it so much.

Without his realizing it after two hours only he and Kathy were left in the pub. They talked about whatever. He told her his life story and she shared hers with him. It was strange but their stories were remarkably alike. Both had lonely childhoods and had been outcasts in school. She had served in the Army as well but felt trapped by the stigmatism of female soldiers.

Kathy asked Charlie to skip Friday's certification dive and join her at DWR access road at Lake Oroville Saturday morning instead for his certification dive. Without questioning he agreed and bid her goodnight. He was shocked to see it dark outside and realized he had never talked to any woman for such a long time. He felt comfortable and warm in the thought of meeting her Saturday for his certification dive.

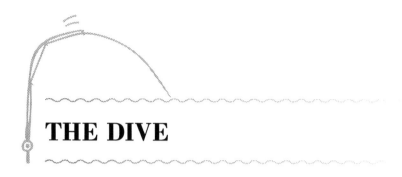

THE DIVE

Saturday arrived hazy due to a forest fire in the area, but Charlie thought it was the most beautiful sunny day he had ever seen. He arrived at the lake and found her waiting for him. They sat and talked for about an hour and finally got into their scuba gear.

Entering the water, they swam together for a while, and she ran him through his paces then they surfaced.

Kathy looked Charlie directly in the eye and said, "Charles, you are now ready for your certification dive." With that she removed her bikini top exposing her breasts to his bugging eyes. She calmly tossed it toward the beach then removed her bottom and sent it to the same locale. Fumbling, Charlie removed his trunks and tossed them to the same place.

The two embraced and Charlie gave and got the greatest kiss of his life. Separating Kathy put her mouthpiece back in and motioned for him to follow. He was an obedient lad and followed her bubble trail.

Fifteen minutes passed with intertwined bubble trails dancing along the water. Suddenly Charlie burst out of the water with the most exuberant shout of joy heard west of the Mississippi in over a century. Euphoria could not describe his feelings. Dismay and shock soon followed.

Kathy surfaced and was puzzled. Charlie was nowhere to be seen. Where could he have gone in such a short time and why? She searched the area to no avail.

EPILOGUE

Lt. Gerrard was shocked by the apparition he faced. He walked around the anomaly trying to comprehend how this could have happened. This was one for the record books.

One naked scuba diver was found in an upright position impaled on a sapling with a most curious cross between a look of glee and surprise pasted on his face.

Charlie was no longer a virgin.

Printed in the United States
by Baker & Taylor Publisher Services